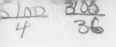

RIVERSIDE PUBLIC LIBRARY FOUNDATION

Community Challenge Campaign
1999

LOUISE
Goes
Wild

by STEPHEN KRENSKY
pictures by SUSANNA NATTI

DIAL BOOKS FOR YOUNG READERS
New York

Published by Dial Books for Young Readers
A division of Penguin Putnam Inc.
345 Hudson Street
New York, New York 10014

Designed by Ann Finnell
Printed in the U.S.A. on acid-free paper
First Edition
1 3 5 7 9 10 8 6 4 2

Library of Congress Cataloging in Publication Data
Krensky, Stephen.
Louise goes wild/by Stephen Krensky; illustrated by Susanna Natti.
—1st ed.
p. cm.
Summary: Tired of being considered predictable, Louise
decides to make some changes in her life, but she finds out
that her family and friends miss the "old Louise"—and so does she.
ISBN 0-8037-2307-5
[1. Identity—Fiction. 2. Self-perception—Fiction.] I. Natti, Susanna, ill.
II. Title.
PZ7.K883Ln 1999 [Fic]—dc21 98-24824 CIP AC

For Julia
S. K.

With love to Alan
S. N.

CHAPTER ONE

"Ridiculous!" said Louise Page as she left the movie theater. "Totally ridiculous."

Her friends Emily and Megan were right behind her.

"I know what you mean," agreed Megan. "That raptor ate the whole frozen food section of the supermarket. He didn't even take the fish sticks out of the boxes."

"No, no," said Louise. "That didn't bother me."

"Oh," said Emily, "then you mean the part where the T-rex brushes his teeth with a pine tree."

Louise shook her head. "That was just

stupid. He didn't even have any toothpaste. No, I couldn't believe the ending."

Emily laughed. "It was mushy. And dinosaur kissing is sort of disgusting."

"True," Louise continued, "but I don't mean that part of the ending. The whole thing was just so *predictable.* I could see it coming a mile away. Even before the raptor trampled the army base."

could happen

"How could you be so sure he was going to escape?" asked Emily. "There were all those soldiers chasing him."

Megan grinned. "The odds of the raptor escaping were 93%."

"That high?"

Megan stopped to think. She had a system for computing the odds of almost anything. "The star of the movie hardly ever dies," she reminded them.

"Well, I still liked the special effects," said Emily, "even without much of a story. They made me hungry."

"Emily," said Megan, "almost everything makes you hungry."

"I know." She paused. "Hey, Louise, can I have one of your Milk Duds?"

Louise stopped walking. "How do you know I have any left?"

"You always save three Milk Duds for the walk home."

"I do?"

Emily nodded. "You're very dependable that way."

"I think you're exaggerating," said Louise, opening the box. "One . . . two . . . Okay, big deal. So this time there happens to be three. Lucky guess." She put one in her mouth.

Emily just smiled. "Whatever you say. So can I have one?"

Louise handed over a Milk Dud. She wasn't happy about it, though. Sharing her candy was fine, but she didn't like the idea that Emily could read her mind.

When Louise got home, she found her younger brother, Lionel, making a snack in the kitchen. Lionel was very fussy about his snacks. This time he was carefully putting two mismatched cookie halves together.

"Where is everybody?" she asked.

"I'm right here," said Lionel.

"I don't mean *you*. I mean everybody else."

"Mom's upstairs."

"Why are you doing that?"

Lionel shrugged. "I'm just experimenting. How was the movie?"

"Same old thing. Dinosaurs trash the world. We trash the dinosaurs."

"Sounds good," Lionel said. "Hey, do you have any Milk Duds left?"

Louise folded her arms. "And why would *you* think that?"

"You always buy Milk Duds at the movies. And you always start home with three—"

"Never mind," said Louise. "I don't want to hear any more about it."

"Touchy," Lionel said. "It was only a question."

"Maybe to you! What is it about everybody and Milk Duds, anyway?"

She did not wait for Lionel to answer. She wasn't really looking for an answer. She just went up to her room. This mind-reading business was getting to be a real pain.

She closed her door and sat on the bed. That was better. Here she had a little privacy. She opened the box and ate her last Milk Dud in peace.

CHAPTER TWO

When the school bell rang on Monday morning, Louise was at her desk, taking homework out of her backpack.

Her teacher, Mr. Hathaway, called for everyone's attention.

"All right, let's settle down. Jasper, I don't believe Brendan will appreciate your tipping his books onto the floor. Please stop pushing them with your ruler."

Reluctantly Jasper put the ruler away.

Mr. Hathaway turned back to the class. "Before we get started, I want to remind everyone that today you can sign up for the school talent show."

A few kids clapped. Others groaned.

"As you know," Mr. Hathaway continued, "the show will feature music, dancing, comedy —whatever you'd like to do. There are no try-outs. Everyone who signs up gets a moment onstage."

Jasper raised his hand.

"Yes, Jasper?"

"I'm thinking of doing a magic act."

Mr. Hathaway opened a book. "I'll look forward to it."

"Well, that's the thing. I thought it would be really good to saw a teacher in half."

"Very ambitious," said Mr. Hathaway. "Of course, your first trick will be finding a teacher to volunteer for the part. Now," he added quickly, "open your science workbooks to page twenty-four. We're going to be studying metamorphosis, specifically how a caterpillar transforms itself into a butterfly."

At recess the talent show was the center of conversation.

"I'm going to do a comedy routine," said Alex.

"You are?" asked Louise. She knew Alex liked to draw. This comedy stuff was something new.

"Sure. Here's one I've been practicing: Do you know where Tarzan works out?"

Louise thought for a moment. "No," she said finally. "Where does Tarzan work out?"

"In a jungle gym!"

Louise rolled her eyes. "Jungle. Gym. Tell

me you didn't make that up yourself. Please."

"Ha, ha. Just wait, Louise. You'll see."

He went off to tell his joke again. Louise ran to catch up with Emily and Megan.

"It's going to take careful timing," said Emily.

Megan agreed. "We should start practicing this afternoon."

"This is about the talent show, right?" Louise asked.

"Don't laugh," said Emily.

"Why should I laugh? You're not planning to saw anybody in half, are you?"

"No way," said Megan. "We're doing a dance thing."

"We didn't ask you to join us," added Emily, "because we know how you feel about being onstage."

Louise shuddered. She hated performing in public. She had played the drums for two years, but never in front of a crowd. Even playing in front of her friends put a tight feeling in her stomach.

She was still curious, though, about what her friends were planning. "What kind of dance thing?" she asked.

"It's complicated," Emily explained. "With music. We haven't worked out all the details."

"Well, good luck," said Louise. "But I wouldn't want to be in your shoes."

Megan shook her head. "The way you dance, Louise, we wouldn't want you in them either."

When the bell rang at the end of the school day, Louise headed for the door.

"Oh, Louise," said Mr. Hathaway, "could you do me a favor?"

"Sure," she said.

"When you're outside playing basketball, could you check on the flowers we planted last week? I want to make certain they're getting enough water."

"Sure, Mr. Hathaway." She started out the door—and then stopped. "Um, Mr. Hathaway, excuse me. . . . How did you know that I was going to play basketball today?"

Mr. Hathaway glanced at the calendar.

"It's Monday, Louise. You always play basketball after school on Mondays."

"I do? Always?"

"You're very reliable, Louise."

Louise wasn't sure if she liked that or not. *Dependable. Reliable.* What did everyone think she was—a computerized robot?

Maybe it was time to write herself a new program.

CHAPTER THREE

When Louise got home from school, she found her mother on the porch.

"Can I ask you something?"

Mrs. Page put down the paper she was reading. "Of course."

"Do you think I'm predictable?"

Her mother considered the question. "Predictable? No, I don't think of you that way. Of course, we all have certain familiar habits. They're part of our personality, our character."

"Uh-huh. But I'm afraid I'm getting a little boring. Everyone else seems to know what I'm going to do even before I know myself."

"I see. Well, that's not all bad. In a way, it's the flip side of having people be able to count on you."

"I suppose. But I'd really like to surprise them now and then."

"Well, if you really want to surprise me, you could start by cleaning your room."

Louise groaned. "Ugh. That's such a *Mom* thing to say."

"All right. Do you want to try a new instrument?"

"No." Louise liked beating on her drums. And even Lionel admitted she was good at it. "But there must be something new I can do."

Her mother smiled. "I understand. You feel like you're in a rut. Don't worry. You've got plenty of changes to look forward to. Just be patient."

Being *patient* was not the kind of advice she was looking for, thought Louise as she headed for the door. Louise had never been patient about anything. And if she was really so predictable, she didn't think this was the time to

17

wait around for a change to just *happen*. No, the time had come to start branching out.

Later that night her father found Louise reading in bed.

"Oh, here you are," he said.

Louise looked up, startled.

"I called to you three times. You didn't answer. That must be a pretty interesting book."

Louise held it up. "It's *The Curse of the Restless Ghost*."

Her father looked surprised. "I thought scary mysteries gave you bad dreams."

Louise waved her hand. "Oh, that was just the old days—when I was little. Now I'm branching out. Moving into new areas. Exploring other dimensions."

Mr. Page scratched his head. "I remember wanting to move into new areas. One time I went to summer camp. . . . Nobody knew me there, so I decided to try on a whole new personality."

"Really?" said Louise. "What did you pick?"

Her father sighed. "I wanted to be a baseball star. It seemed like a good idea at first. Of course, there were problems. . . the big one being that I wasn't very athletic."

"So what happened?"

"Well, I had hinted to the other kids about my skills without being too specific. It was just as well. In my first game I struck out three times." He winced at the memory. "So I went back to being plain old me. It wasn't perfect, but I was a lot more comfortable."

Louise frowned. "I don't need to be a sports star, but I don't want to be plain old me either."

"Okay, but just remember, we like the plain old you pretty well."

Much later, when everyone was supposed to be asleep, Louise tiptoed into Lionel's room.

"Lionel!" she whispered.

"Hmmmmph."

"Lionel, wake up! Do you hear something?"

Lionel opened his eyes. "I hear you shouting in my ear, Louise. But it can't be the real you. This is my room, and it's the middle of the night. I must still be sleeping." He pinched Louise's nose. "Very lifelike, though."

He rolled over.

Louise shook his shoulder. "Lionel, you're not dreaming. I really am here."

Lionel yawned. "Stop shaking me. I believe you. But why? Did you have a bad dream?"

Louise glanced around. "No, no, I haven't been to sleep yet."

Lionel looked at his clock. "But it's after midnight."

"I know. I just wasn't tired."

"You were reading that book—*Ghost Curse* or whatever."

"Yes, I was."

"Was it spooky?"

"I guess. I've been trying not to think about it too much. Then I heard some noises. . . ."

Lionel sat up. "What kind of noises?"

"Well, there was scratching outside my window. And a kind of howling."

"What about under your bed?"

"Under my bed? No, I didn't notice anything there."

"That's where I always hear noises first," Lionel went on. "I'm not sure who lives under there. Sometimes I think they go away on vacation for a while. Then they come back and bother me again."

"Lionel, this is no time to worry about what goes on under your bed. It's *me* we're talking about."

"Oh. I forgot." Lionel yawned. "Well, you could open your window to see what's out there."

"Is that really safe?"

Lionel didn't know. "It might just be a branch scratching the house."

"I guess," said Louise.

"Or it might be a ghost scratching itself."

"Ghosts don't scratch themselves," said Louise.

"They do if they're itchy."

"Thanks, Lionel. You're a big help."

"I do my best," he said. "Good night."

Louise returned to her room. Shadows danced outside her curtains. She tried turning to the wall, but then she couldn't watch the door. Who knew what might sneak up on her if she wasn't looking? But even with her back to the wall, she wasn't safe. A ghost could pass right through the wall and grab her from behind.

In the end she pulled the blanket over her head and huddled in a ball. When she finally fell asleep, she dreamed of itchy ghosts till morning.

CHAPTER FOUR

"Come on, Louise!" her mother shouted up the stairs.

"In a minute!"

Mrs. Page sat down at the breakfast table with Lionel.

"Is your homework in your backpack?" she asked.

"I think so."

"Well, check before you go out." She looked at the stairs. "I wonder what's taking Louise so long."

"She's probably tired," said Lionel. "I know she didn't sleep well."

Mr. Page walked in with the newspaper.

"Is Louise still up in the bathroom? She's been there forever—which even for her is a long time."

He looked down at the table.

"Who's eating the Krunchy Munchies?" He looked at the wall calendar. "Oh, it's Tuesday. They must be for Louise. That girl runs like clockwork." He checked his watch. "Of course, sometimes it's slow clockwork."

Louise came in. "Good morning, everyone!"

Everyone stared at her.

"Sorry I'm late. I sure am hungry, though. I'm going to have some toast and half a grapefruit."

Everyone was still staring.

"I'll just put back the Krunchy Munchies. Thanks anyway, Lionel. But I do like *some* variety."

Mr. Page coughed. "We can see that."

"Oh, this?" Louise patted her hair. "I saw it in a magazine. Thought I'd try something new."

"Your hair is all curls, Louise," said Lionel. "Does it hurt?"

"No, don't be silly. I planned it this way."

Lionel's mouth dropped open. "You mean you did it on purpose?"

"Honestly, Lionel, you're such a child sometimes. These curls are the latest thing."

Mrs. Page nodded slowly. "I can see you worked hard on this new look."

"Very hard. I practically wore out your curling iron. Do you like it?"

"Um . . . it's certainly distinctive."

Louise smiled. "See, Lionel?"

He was not convinced. "How are you going to change it before we have to leave for school? There isn't much time."

"Change it? I wasn't planning to change it."

Now Lionel was really impressed. "Gee, Louise," he said, "you're braver than I thought."

It didn't take long for the kids at school to notice the new Louise.

Alex's eyes opened very wide at his first glimpse. "That's amazing, Louise. Your hair looks just like a collection of corkscrews."

"So you don't think they're too springy?"

"Well, you have to experiment with things before getting them right." He grinned. "And sometimes that's the most fun."

"Fun? What fun?" said Jasper, coming around the corner. Megan and Lauren were right behind him.

"Whoa!" said Jasper. "I see the circus is in town. What happened to you, Louise? Stick your finger in an electrical socket?"

"No, no," Megan said. "An electrical shock wouldn't affect her hair like that."

"That's right," said Lauren. "Electricity makes your hair stick out straight in all directions. I've seen it in cartoons."

"Okay," said Jasper. "But it still must have been some sort of terrible accident. Right, Louise? Tell us the gory details."

Louise wasn't pleased with the direction the conversation was going.

"It wasn't an accident at all," she explained. "I did this to my hair on purpose."

Jasper clutched his chest.

Louise gave him a look. "At least I'm not afraid to take chances."

"We can certainly *see* that," said Megan. "How long will this, um, chance last?"

Louise wasn't sure. "Until I take a shower, I think."

"Will you be doing that soon?"

"We'll see," said Louise. "We'll see."

CHAPTER FIVE

By the end of the day Louise knew that her hair experiment had failed. Creating change was important, but hearing everybody snicker behind her back was not the sort of change she was aiming for.

So the next day the curls were gone. But she wasn't done yet.

It took a few days, though, to plan her next attempt. When she came down to breakfast the following Wednesday, she was wearing her long raincoat.

Lionel gave her a strange look. "Where's your umbrella?" he asked.

"Ha, ha. I heard it might rain later."

"Indoors?"

"I'm just trying to be prepared."

"Come on, Louise. What's going on?"

Louise sighed. "All right, all right." She took off the raincoat.

Lionel gasped. "What happened to your clothes?"

"Nothing."

"How can you say *nothing*?"

"Lionel, I hardly expect you to show any fashion sense."

"That's for sure. I don't even know what fashion sense is."

"Keep an open mind, Lionel. Obviously you don't know everything about me. You've only seen the surface. Underneath I'm a woman of mystery."

At that moment Mrs. Page entered the kitchen. "Is everyone—Louise, what is that you're wearing?"

"My *clothes*, Mother. What else would they be?"

Mrs. Page looked at her skeptically. "Were your eyes open the whole time? I've never seen orange and hot pink combined like that. Especially with lime green pants."

"I know you were expecting the usual from me. But I no longer do the expected."

"She's a woman of mystery," Lionel explained.

"I see," Mrs. Page said politely. "Well, I suppose the choice is yours. But don't you have a field trip today?"

"Yes. We're going to the aquarium. They have a new fish tank."

"Who has a new fish tank?" asked Mr. Page, coming down the stairs. He stopped short, staring at Louise.

"What happened here? Was there an accident?"

"It's just Louise's woman-of-mystery look," Lionel explained.

"Oh." Mr. Page walked slowly around his daughter. "I knew there had to be a logical explanation."

Louise was getting mad. She didn't appreciate all these careful comments.

"This whole family's in a rut!" she shouted. "And I don't want to be in it with you."

"Calm down, honey," said her mother.

"You're turning red," Lionel told her. "It doesn't go with the other colors."

Louise clenched her fists.

"You all need imagination transplants, that's what you need!"

She tromped down the stairs and out the door.

Louise got to school long before the first bell. But she was not the only one there. A lot of kids were arriving early to practice in the auditorium for the talent show.

Louise hung up her coat and went to watch.

"Hi, Louise," said Matthew. "I didn't know you were in the talent show. That's quite a costume. Are you some kind of medieval court jester?"

"No," said Louise.

"A box of crayons?"

"No. If you must know, this isn't a costume. These clothes are not part of any act. I just decided to wear them today."

Matthew gaped at her. "You're kidding."

Louise went nose to nose with him. "Do I look like I'm kidding?"

Matthew hastily retreated. "Can't say that you do. Bye."

Up on the stage several acts were practicing

at once. Some third graders were jumping Double Dutch while another group was turning somersaults.

Emily and Megan were working off to one side. Both girls were concentrating very hard. Emily was tap dancing around Megan in a circle while Megan waved a streamer on a stick over both girls' heads. The streamer, though, kept brushing Emily's face.

"That tickles," she said.

"Sorry," said Megan. She looked up. "Oh, hi, Louise." She took another look. "What happened to you?"

"I like it," said Emily. "I can't wear orange. It makes me look pale. But on you it's bold, it's daring, it's . . ."

"Hard on the eyes," said Megan.

"That's the bold part," Emily reminded her.

"Well," said Louise, "I'm glad somebody has the sense to . . ."

At that moment a group of kindergartners came into the auditorium. They were going to rehearse a dance around a maypole on the stage. But once they saw Louise's clothes, they flocked over to her.

"Look! A giant flower!" they shouted. "Giant flower!"

"No, wait," said Louise. "There's been a mistake."

The little children started to sing. Then they began running around Louise, wrapping her in crepe paper.

"Now I see what you mean, Emily," said Megan. "That's bold, all right."

Louise just sighed.

CHAPTER SIX

The bus ride to the aquarium went fairly quickly. Almost everyone was in a good mood because any time away from school was time well spent. The ride itself was considered a success because the kids were able to get three truck drivers to blow their horns at them.

The aquarium was a big concrete building with large round windows like giant portholes in a ship. It was built on the edge of the harbor. There were docks on either side and an outdoor pool where seals performed in the summer.

The children went inside, where they

looked at some exhibits along the wall. There were examples of life in marshes and ponds and a cutaway view of life on the ocean floor.

Jasper pressed his nose against the glass of the main tank.

"Glub," he said to the dogfish on the other side. "Glub, glub."

"I think it understands you," said Louise.

"Really?" said Jasper.

She nodded solemnly.

"MAY I HAVE YOUR ATTENTION, PLEASE!" The aquarium guide called them over to a collection of sunken pools and rocks surrounded by a high wall. "This is our penguin habitat."

The guide went on to tell them all about penguins—how they ate underwater and slept standing up.

"Actually, you're here at a good time," the guide explained. She held up a bucket full of small fish. "The penguins are about to have lunch. Does anyone want to help feed them?"

Louise raised her hand.

Emily pulled it down. *"Louise!"* she hissed. *"You're going to have to hold those fish. You hate slimy things."*

Louise reminded herself that this was something she absolutely positively would not have done before. "It's okay, Emily. Really."

"Excellent," said the guide. She gave Louise's clothes a good look. "The penguins should have no trouble picking you out."

She handed Louise two rubber gloves and a bucket of fish.

The smell was awful.

Louise wrinkled her nose. "Should I just dump the bucket out?"

"No, no. We don't want the penguins rushing together. You have to scatter the fish around."

Too bad, thought Louise. She put on the gloves. Then she reached gingerly into the pail and pulled out some fish. Even with gloves on, she could tell how slippery they were.

"Don't be shy," said the guide. "Get a little closer." She opened a gate for Louise to pass through.

Louise inched down two steps and onto a rock. The penguins in their tuxedoes looked at her with hungry interest. They made her feel like a waiter in a fancy restaurant.

"Just a little closer," said the guide.

As Louise reached again into the pail, one of the penguins flapped suddenly. Some of the water hit Louise. It was cold, and she instinctively jumped back. The rock was slippery, though, and she lost her balance.

"Whoooaaaa!" cried Louise.

She slid off the rock and into the water. Everyone gasped.

Most of the penguins scattered as Louise splashed into their midst. A few brave ones came forward to eat the fish that had emptied out of the bucket.

The guide climbed down to her side and reached out an arm to help her up. "Are you all right?"

Louise wasn't sure. She was definitely wet. Then she shivered.

"Are you cold? The water isn't heated."

"Not cold. I . . ." Louise reached into her shirt and pulled out one of the fish.

"Yuck!"

A few of the kids screamed.

Mr. Hathaway rushed over to check on her. "Louise, are you all right? That was quite a spill."

"I'm fine," said Louise. "Really. Well, I'm wet . . ." She took a deep breath. "And stinky. But I'm not hurt."

While everyone else ate lunch, Louise washed up in the bathroom. The aquarium gave her a sweat suit from the gift shop and a bag for her wet clothes.

A certain fishy smell, though, still clung to her.

"Making changes is not going the way I expected," she muttered to Emily as they boarded the bus.

"Look on the bright side. Nobody will want to sit with you on the ride back. You'll have a whole seat to yourself."

Louise groaned. "I feel better already."

CHAPTER SEVEN

"Tell it again," said Lionel.

Louise shook her head. "Lionel, I've told you a million times already."

"I know, but I love the part where the fish goes down your shirt. I could hear that part all day."

"Enough, Lionel," said Mrs. Page. "Let's not dwell on the past. That was three days ago. Concentrate on the menu."

The Pages had gone out to dinner at a Chinese restaurant. It was a family tradition that they each picked one item, and then everyone shared.

"Sizzling Rice Soup with chicken," said

Lionel. "That's what I want."

"Big surprise," said Louise. "You always order that."

"I know what I like."

"So do I," said Mr. Page. "Scallion pancakes."

"Beef with snow peas for me," said Mrs. Page. "What about you, Louise?"

Louise stared at the menu.

Lionel laughed. "What's the big decision?

You always get lemon chicken."

"Not tonight. I want to try something new. Different." She glanced at the menu. "Kung Pao chicken, maybe."

Mr. Page looked concerned. "Louise, that's listed in red ink. With stars. Red ink means it's hot. The stars mean super hot."

Louise didn't care. "Well, I like hot things."

"We're not talking about the beach, Louise. This is food."

"Maybe I didn't like hot and spicy food before," Louise admitted. "But a person can change."

Her father shrugged. "All right. It's your choice."

While they were waiting for their order, Lionel told them about his friend Jeffrey's act for the talent show.

"He's going to balance an egg on the tip of his nose."

"What kind of talent is that?" asked Louise.

"A really special one. It's not a talent you see every day."

Mr. Page wriggled his nose back and forth. "I guess not."

When the Pages' food arrived, Mr. and Mrs. Page passed around the dishes.

"Will you try some of the Kung Pao?" Mrs. Page asked Lionel.

He looked at it suspiciously. "What are those things that look like burnt worms?"

"Peppers," said his mother. "You don't eat them. They're just for flavoring."

"No way," said Lionel.

"Don't be such a baby," said Louise. "Look, I'll show you." She stuck one in her mouth.

"Ah . . . Louise," her father began, "that may not be—"

"This is the new Louise you're talking to. I'm not afraid of a shriveled pepper."

Her mother sighed.

Louise kept chewing. "This isn't so bad. I

don't see what all the fuss is about. These things are—"

She suddenly stopped talking.

"Louise, you look funny," Lionel said.

"Water!" she hissed.

Louise's eyes welled up. A moment later tears were streaming down her cheeks.

Her father motioned to the waiter. "We'll need water here. And keep it coming!"

Louise spit the pepper into her napkin.

"Is she going to be all right?" Lionel asked.

"Eventually," said her mother, passing her water glass to Louise.

"Okay, then," said Lionel. He leaned back to enjoy the show.

When the Pages got home, Louise went straight to the basement. At the restaurant she had swallowed water, rice, and juice followed by two bowls of sherbet. Her mouth wasn't burning anymore, but the memory was still very fresh.

She started playing her drums to take her mind off her mouth. The faster she played, the better she felt.

"Louise, we need to talk."

Her mother was standing in the doorway.

At least Louise knew she wasn't in trouble. Her parents thought that she had been punished enough for acting so rashly.

Mrs. Page sat down. "How are you feeling?"

"Better."

"Good. I want you to know, Louise, that I admire your wish to stir up your life. But maybe you should think things through a little more."

"Oh?"

Her mother smiled. "You've been concentrating on changing the outer you, the surface. I know that's the part people see, and it's the part you would naturally think of first. But real change comes from within. It doesn't come from what you look like or what you eat. It comes from what you believe and how you act on those beliefs."

Louise thought this over. She had to admit that changing the outside stuff was not working the way she had planned. Maybe starting from the inside would be better.

"But what kind of inside thing should I start with?"

"That's for you to decide," her mother said. "But don't try to change too many things at once. Concentrate on one part of yourself at a time. And don't be in too big a hurry to change. Some things are meant to take time."

Louise thought about all this as she went upstairs to bed. It was hard to think about changing her inside. She didn't even know what her inside looked like. Was she a mess on the inside, or was she very organized? If she made changes, she'd be doing it blindly.

And how much change was enough? It was all very confusing.

When she finally fell asleep, she was curled up like a giant question mark.

CHAPTER EIGHT

Watching the talent show from the bleachers, Louise thought the gym was beginning to look like a country fair. There were jugglers on one side and joke tellers on the other. Several first and second graders were taking turns playing the piano.

Everyone was talking at once.

"Why did the hen boast that she could lay an egg as big as a house?" said Alex.

"Why?" Louise asked.

"Because she liked to *eggs*-aggerate."

In the middle of the stage Jasper was working on his magic act.

"Hmmm," said Brendan. "I see Jasper's

still having trouble finding a partner to make disappear."

"Maybe he could make himself disappear," said Lauren. "I'd *pay* to see that."

Brendan folded his arms. "Come on, Jasper, hurry up!"

"Show some respect," said Jasper. "I am now The Amazing Jasper."

Brendan tried to keep a straight face.

"As you know," The Amazing Jasper went on, "things like to grow in the spring. One day there are just some green shoots in the ground, and then before you know it"—Jasper waved his arms—"out come the flowers.

"*Presto!*" The Amazing Jasper tried to pull a bouquet out of thin air. Actually, the flowers were hidden up his sleeve. Unfortunately they snagged on a shirt button on the way out.

Jasper sighed.

"Keep trying, Jasper," called out Louise. "You'll get the hang of it."

Jasper smiled. "Thanks, Louise. Hey, I was wondering, would you like to help The

Amazing Jasper in the show?"

Louise considered it. Nobody would expect her to team up with Jasper.

"Would I be The Amazing Louise?"

"No, you'd be the ordinary assistant. The act can only have one star."

"Oh. Well, thanks anyway, Jasper."

Even though Louise didn't accept The Amazing Jasper's offer, it still started her thinking. She had not considered being in the show, but maybe she should. Just the idea of performing put a knot in her stomach. That told her that this would be a change starting on the inside. But where could she find a place for herself?

"You want to *what*?" Emily's mouth dropped open.

"I want to be in your act," said Louise.

Megan looked stunned. "It would not have occurred to me to figure those odds at all. So what do you plan on doing?"

"I'm not sure," Louise admitted. Sometimes her unpredictability ran ahead of the rest of her. "It's a dance routine, right?"

"Partly."

"Well, then, I'll dance, of course."

Louise could see that Emily was trying not to make a face. Louise was not known as the best dancer. Her legs were always getting tangled up.

"In front of everyone?" Emily asked. "Onstage?"

"Naturally," said Louise. "Where else would I go?"

"But you hate performing!"

"I fed the fish to the penguins, didn't I? That was in front of everyone."

"True," said Megan. "But look what happened. The penguins almost ate *you* for lunch."

"That wasn't my fault. Anyway, there's no water in your act. I should be perfectly safe."

"You're our friend, Louise," Megan said. "We don't want to leave you out. But this will be a lot of work."

"No problem."

"And you have to sing."

"Okay."

"And there are the costumes," added Emily.

"Costumes? What costumes?"

"We haven't made them yet," Emily explained. "But we're planning to make up something with tassels."

"Tassels? You mean those dangly pieces that hang from a skirt or something?"

"Exactly."

Louise frowned. She hated tassels. At least the old Louise hated tassels. They looked so frilly.

"Do we have to?"

Megan folded her arms. "Remember, Louise, you asked to be in *our* act. We didn't ask to be in *yours*."

"You're right. I'm sorry."

The new Louise would not shrink from tassels. The more tassels, the better.

But if she was lucky, no one would recognize her.

CHAPTER NINE

Normally Louise liked going to Emily's house after school. It was a good place to talk and Emily's mother did not believe that fruit was a real after-school snack. And while Emily had a brother too, he was in eighth grade and just ignored them. This was a little insulting, perhaps, but it kept everything very peaceful. At her house it was rarely peaceful with Lionel around.

However, after several afternoon rehearsals even Emily's house was a lot less fun. Louise's toes hurt and her knees creaked from all the bending and twisting.

One week before the talent show she was

down in Emily's basement practicing with both her partners.

"Let's pick it up from the last measure," said Emily. She put on the tape.

Louise tried to sway in step with the music. Her head could follow the rhythm, but her feet were clearly not paying enough attention. And the scarf she was waving over her head kept tickling her nose.

Left foot, then right. Or was it right foot,

then left? Jump—Leap—Jump. Or was it Leap—Jump—Leap? She didn't know. Her feet didn't know either.

Louise slumped to the floor.

"Don't give up," said Megan.

Louise rubbed her leg. "I just have a cramp."

"You know, Louise," said Emily, "we understand that you haven't had as much time to practice as we've had. You'll catch on soon enough."

Megan was calculating. "We only seem to be executing 63% of our movements in sync with the music."

"I'm messing you up, aren't I?" said Louise.

"No," said Megan. "I'm not comfortable yet myself. We wanted to mix music and dance and a little gymnastics, but we're not mixing as well as I'd hoped. Do you have any ideas how we could make it better?"

Louise hesitated. The old Louise always had more ideas than she knew what to do with. And the old Louise wasn't shy about sharing them. But now she was the new Louise. Besides, she was sort of a guest in this act. It was better to keep still.

"I think it's coming along," she said, hoping there wouldn't be any other questions. She looked quickly at her watch. "Oh, it's getting late. I need to get home to help make dinner. It's my week."

Emily smiled. "What happens when it's Lionel's week?"

Louise made a face. "I lose weight," she said.

When she got to her house, her father was cleaning green beans in the kitchen. He pointed toward the sink.

"Potatoes," he said.

While Louise was rinsing them off, she looked them over. It was interesting about potatoes. From a distance they all looked the same. But up close each one had different bumps and ridges.

"How's your act coming along?" her father asked.

Louise wasn't sure. "Well, it was really nice of Emily and Megan to let me join in."

"Yes . . . yes it was. But are you enjoying yourself? I didn't know you liked to dance. I guess you really are a woman of mystery."

Louise almost smiled. "A tired woman of mystery," she said.

"Well, don't get too mysterious. Copying your friends may not be the answer you're looking for."

Louise cut up the potatoes and spread them out on a baking sheet. "It's not that I want to copy them exactly," she said. "I'm just tired of copying myself."

Her father took the chicken out of the oven to baste it. "That's a worthy goal, Louise, but you don't want to make changes without thinking them through. Stretching yourself is one thing. Making a complete break is another."

Louise coated the potatoes with olive oil and seasoned them with salt and pepper. "But how do you tell the difference?" she asked.

"It's tricky," he said. "Partly it's a feeling of pressure. If you try to fit into a new shape and you feel squeezed or pulled too tightly, then you need to back off. There's a lot of trial and error. With a little luck, you'll figure it out eventually."

Luck would be good, thought Louise. She put the potatoes in the oven and went off to set the table.

CHAPTER TEN

When Louise got to school the next morning, she could see that all was not well. Emily was sitting at her desk, ripping a piece of paper into smaller and smaller pieces. Emily only did that when things were bad.

Even worse, Megan was sitting beside her, handing over more paper as needed.

"What's wrong?" Louise asked.

"Emily heard some of the other kids talking about our act," said Megan. "Jasper said we looked like butterflies with our heads cut off."

"Ouch!" said Louise.

"And that was one of the nicer comments."

Megan sighed. "There was also some stuff about dancing at sea during an earthquake and how our long scarves remind everyone of toilet paper unrolling."

"Double ouch!" said Louise.

"There's more."

Louise sat down to listen.

"The worst thing," said Megan, "is that we kind of agree. The act isn't working yet. At this point we feel there's a 76% chance we'll be laughed off the stage."

"I don't think they allow that," said Louise.

"Maybe not," said Megan. "But that's how we feel." She looked hard at Louise. "What do you think?"

"Oh, I'm trying not to think so much. I used to do too much of that."

This was not entirely true. Lately Louise had realized that all this changing was a lot more complicated than she had expected. She wanted to be different, but she had hoped that the difference would start to feel natural. The way she felt now, it was as if she were wearing someone else's clothes—and they were always too big or too small. She was beginning to miss the old Louise, even if her life had held fewer surprises. Surprises, Louise had found, were not always a good thing.

"That's what we want to talk to you about," said Emily. "We need you, Louise."

Louise was glad. It was good to be needed.

"But . . ." added Megan.

"But what?"

"We need the old Louise to figure out how to fix the act. The dependable, reliable, always-in-charge Louise. It's not that we don't like this new you. I mean you're exciting this way too. But we just need the old you."

Louise hesitated. "I don't know . . ." she began.

"Come on, Louise. We know you can do it."

"There isn't much time. . . ."

"Think of it as a challenge."

"All right," said Louise. "You've talked me into it." A big shudder passed through her body and she threw up her hands. "Okay, I'm *back*."

"Hooray!" said Megan. "My day just improved 13%."

Louise laughed. "Only 13%?"

"The day is young," said Megan.

"So," said Emily, "do you have any ideas?"

Louise shrugged. "Maybe one or two."

"Go on," said Megan.

"Okay. The first thing we have to do is change the costumes. These scarves are too long. I don't know about you, but I worry about tripping over them. As for those tassels . . ." She wrinkled her nose. "The second thing is the music. We need a harder edge. We want to grab their attention and shake it till they cry for mercy."

"We do?" said Emily.

"Well, something like that. . . ."

Her friends smiled. For someone who hadn't been thinking about changing the act, Louise certainly had a lot to say.

CHAPTER ELEVEN

"Moo!" said Lionel.

He and his parents were filing into the school auditorium. Louise was already backstage with all the other performers.

"Moo!" Lionel said again.

"Why do you keep saying that?" his father asked. "Don't tell me you're changing too?"

"No, no. I just feel like a cow being herded in the roundup."

They shuffled forward.

"I see what you mean," said Mr. Page. "Moooo!"

Mrs. Page gave him a look.

He decided to change the subject. "Do you

think the girls are ready?" he asked. "I understand they changed the act a lot in the last few
days."

"Oh, no," said Lionel. "Not more change."

"I think this was a change for the better,"
said his mother. "At least Louise seemed
more comfortable."

Behind the stage curtain Louise stood huddled with Emily and Megan.

"Are you nervous?" Emily asked.

Megan nodded. "There's a 100% chance of

complete and total nervousness. What about you, Louise?"

"The old me might have been a little nervous."

"And the *new* old you?"

Louise giggled. "Absolutely *petrified*."

The talent show was organized very loosely. The acts were spread out so that there were never too many singers, or comedians or other similar acts bunched together. The only firm rule was that the kindergarten children went first because they got too excited to wait any longer.

Alex went on after all the kindergartners were done.

"Which letter of the alphabet do fish like best?" he asked the audience.

Nobody knew.

"The *C*. Get it? Sea."

The audience groaned and clapped.

"Why do young chickens go to school?" Alex went on.

Nobody knew.

"To get a good *egg*-ucation."

Once Alex finished his routine, some family jugglers tossed around plastic bowling pins and a singing trio performed "Take Me Out to the Ball Game." Then Jasper appeared on the stage. He was wearing dark clothes, a top hat, and a cape. In one hand he held a white-tipped magic wand.

"Good evening," he said, raising his arms. "I am The Amazing Jasper. I wanted to cut someone in half tonight. I have the saw," he added, pulling it out from under his cloak. *"But no volunteers."*

Everyone laughed.

Jasper put down the saw.

"The truth is, I had a lot of trouble getting an assistant to appear with me at all. But I finally found one. Behold!"

He took off his hat and pulled out a rabbit.

"This is Esmerelda." Jasper patted his hair. "Luckily," he said, "she just sat quietly up there."

Everyone laughed again.

"Esmerelda is a very busy rabbit. She has a lot of other appearances to make tonight. So I'm just going to send her on her way."

He carefully lowered the rabbit into a box on the table beside him.

"Good-bye, Esmerelda. Thanks for coming."

He put the lid on the box and spun it around.

"One, two, three!"

He opened the box and lifted it up.

The rabbit was gone.

The audience applauded, and Jasper took a bow.

When the curtain opened again, Louise was sitting alone on the stage with her drums. As she slowly tapped out a steady beat, Emily and Megan entered from the left and right. They both wore cone-shaped hats and had red circles painted on their cheeks.

As Louise sped up her tapping, Emily and Megan moved about. Their arms and legs matched the rhythm of the drumbeats as they

moved across the stage. When the girls turned to the side, the audience could see giant keys sticking out of their backs.

Lionel nudged his mother. "The keys make them look like windup toys," he whispered.

She nodded. "That's the idea. Who do you think sewed the keys onto the back of the costumes?"

As the beat quickened, Emily and Megan whirled faster around the stage. Then, as the beat slowed again, they slowed as well. Finally they fell into a heap in the middle of the stage.

Louise then stood up, walked forward in a jerky motion, and fell on top of them—showing the key in her back too.

As the curtain closed, the applause started up—and Louise slowly began to smile.

CHAPTER TWELVE

The talent show was a big success. Backstage, everyone was congratulating one another.

"Great jokes!"

"Nice cartwheels!"

"I can't believe you really threw a pie in your mother's face."

Emily and Megan were removing their cone hats.

"Uh-oh," said Emily, looking over Louise's shoulder. "Trouble coming our way."

Jasper walked over, still wearing his hat and cape. He made a deep bow.

"I didn't think you guys could do it," he admitted.

"And what do you think now?" asked Emily.

Jasper jerked his arms up and down and clapped his hands together.

"Well, you were pretty amazing too," said Megan. "Where did you ever find that rabbit?"

"It's my cousin's. That reminds me. I left her nibbling some lettuce in her cage. I'd better go check on her."

Louise put her arms around her friends' shoulders. "So, are we ready for the bright lights, the big city? Broadway? Hollywood?"

"Watch out, world," said Emily. "She's *really* back."

"No doubt about it," added Megan.

Louise smiled. She might be the old Louise in some ways, but not everything was the same. She had learned a lot from stirring things up. For one thing, there was no single big change that would suddenly make her life perfect. As Alex had said, she would just have to experiment here and there. Sometimes

that might be a little scary, but it certainly wouldn't be boring. And sooner or later, she'd figure out what changes suited her best. Her father had been right about that.

"Here comes your family," said Emily. "Are you going to tell them the news—the old Louise has returned?"

"Eventually," said Louise. "But I want to drive them a little crazier first."

After all, sometimes change was good.